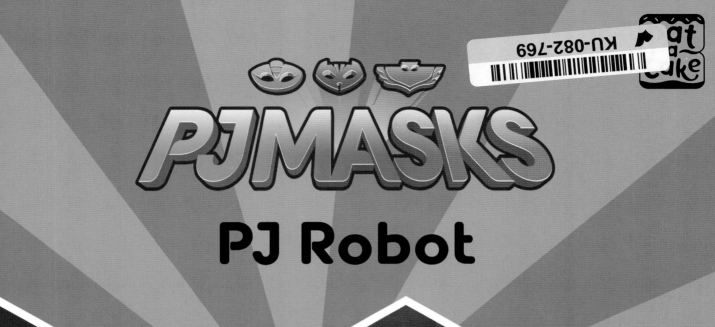

PJ MASKS

PJ Robot

Romeo was working on a new
gadget. The PJ Masks watched
from the shadows.
"I've done it!" cackled the baddie.
"My best invention ever!"
"What is he up to this time?"
whispered Catboy.

Noticing the heroes,
Romeo scurried back
into his Lab.
"Nothing to do with you,
PJ Pests!" he glared.

The next day, Connor and his friends studied the pieces of metal Romeo had left behind.

"His 'best' invention ever . . ." said Amaya.

"That means his horriblest invention ever," frowned Connor.

"We've got to stop him!"

PJ MASKS ARE ON THEIR WAY, INTO THE NIGHT TO SAVE THE DAY!

NIGHT IN THE CITY. A BRAVE BAND OF HEROES IS READY TO FACE FIENDISH VILLAINS TO STOP THEM MESSING WITH YOUR DAY.

AMAYA BECOMES . . . *OWLETTE!*

CONNOR BECOMES . .

CATBOY!

GREG BECOMES... GEKKO!

The PJ Masks rushed to the Cat-Car. They had to track down Romeo's Lab!
When they found the Lab, it was making some very strange noises.

BANG! CRASH! SPARK!

"What's he doing in there?" wondered Gekko.

Suddenly, the Lab door opened and a tiny robot floated out!
It gave each of the heroes a friendly hug.
"That's a cool invention!" said Catboy. "A brand-new mini-bot."
"Aww," chuckled Gekko. "It's so cute!"

Owlette was worried. "Why would Romeo invent a robot that is nice?"
Catboy's ears started to twitch.
Something wasn't right.
"Wait!" he warned.
"I hear voices!"

"Super Cat Ears!"

The hero tracked the sounds. It didn't take Catboy long to find Romeo, showing off to his robot helpers.

"Wait 'til they totally love the mini-bot and take it back to their HQ," boasted Romeo. "Then I'll use the Robot Controller to make it do what I say." Catboy gasped. The mini-bot was a trap!

Catboy raced back to warn the others. Romeo came scuttling after him.
"You blew my plans!" he bellowed. "I'm taking the mini-bot back."
Romeo pressed a button on his Robot Controller **ZAP!**

The mini-bot came back to Romeo, trapped in the Robot Controller's beam.

"Poor little guy," said Owlette.
"It does what I say!" shouted Romeo, but he got so carried away with pushing buttons, the Robot Controller slipped out of his hand!
Catboy picked it up.
"Hey, little robot," said Gekko. "How about hanging out with us?"

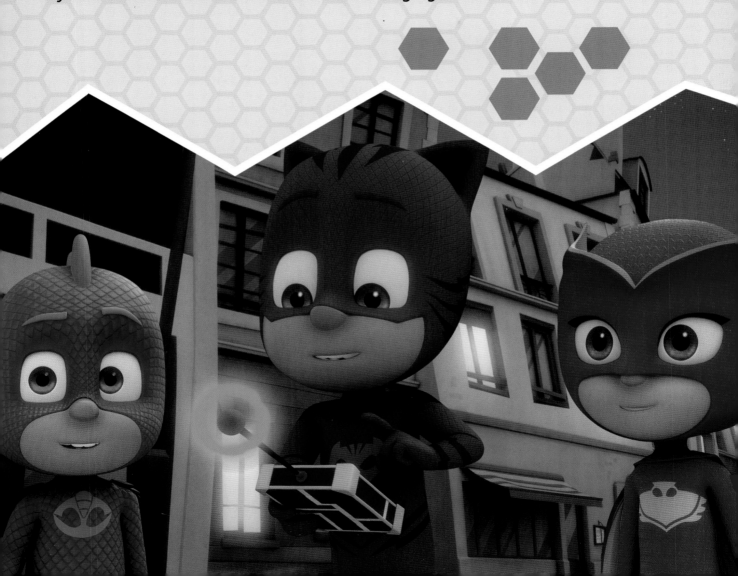

Catboy freed the mini-bot, then whisked him to safety.

"Noooo!" wailed Romeo.

The villain sobbed like a baby . . . until the PJ Masks were out of sight.

"Ha ha!" he laughed, as soon as the coast was clear. "My plan is working!"

The PJ Masks couldn't wait to show the mini-bot around their HQ.
"You can help out around here," suggested Gekko.

The mini-bot got to work. First, he polished the Gekko-Mobile until
it was Super Lizard Shiny. Then he did some Cat Speed practice with Catboy.

"The mini-bot really does seem to like us," said Owlette, turning on the PJ Picture Player.

The mini-bot gazed at the screen in wonder.

"Cool seeing all these pictures, huh?" nodded Gekko.

A picture popped up of the PJ Masks dressed in their suits.

"There's us," said Catboy. "Heading out to save the day . . ."

The mini-bot clapped his hands, then hovered in the air like a hero.

"He doesn't just want to help us," gasped Catboy.

"He wants to **be** one of us!"

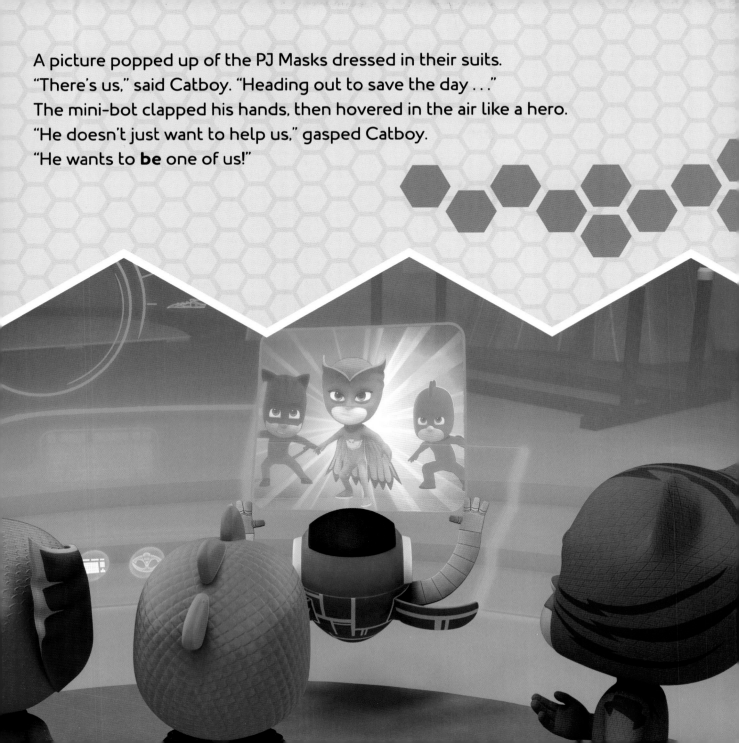

The mini-bot bleeped in surprise. A new picture flashed up on screen –
it showed Romeo in the park, inventing again!
Catboy and Owlette went to check out what Romeo was up to.
"Oh no," whispered Owlette. "He's built a SUPER Robot Controller.
He's going to use it to control the mini-bot."

So that was Romeo's next move! The heroes rushed back to warn Gekko.

Back at HQ, Gekko had been doing some painting.
"Look at little robot!" he cried. "He's got special PJ colours.
He's a PJ Robot now!"

PJ Robot looked like a true hero.

"He's part of the team," said Gekko. "Checking out the vehicles, exploring HQ . . ."

"What if Romeo gets hold of him again?" asked Owlette.

Gekko was confused. The PJ Masks had the Robot Controller already.

"Romeo has built a new one," explained Catboy. "And it's BIG."

The heroes were agreed. They needed to get the Super Robot Controller.
"Romeo could use it to destroy our HQ," said Catboy. "Let's go!"
Owlette picked up the small controller.
"I'll bring this with us," she decided.

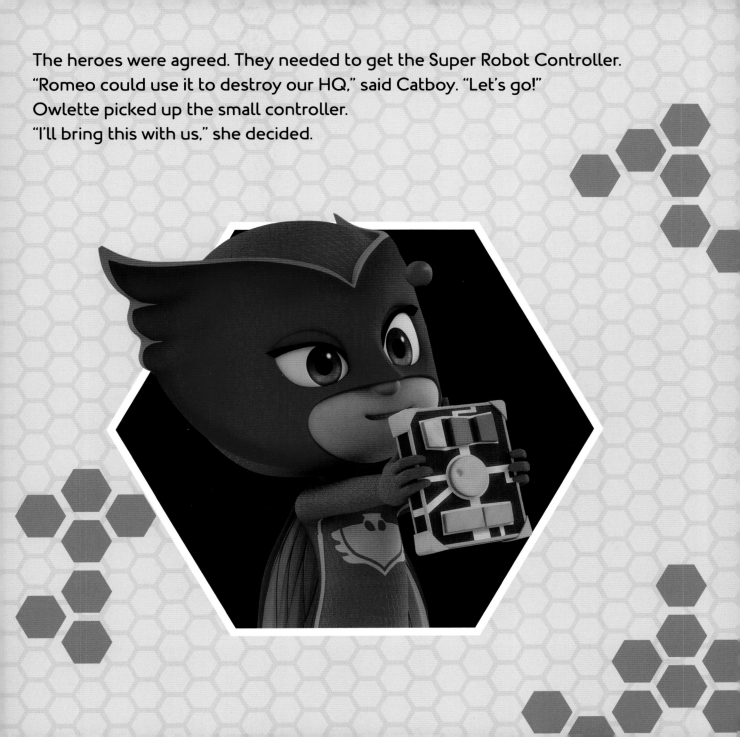

The PJ Masks zoomed to the park in the Cat-Car. Catboy, Gekko and
Owlette hid PJ Robot out of sight, then stepped forwards.
Owlette pointed up at the Super Robot Controller.
"It's aimed at us!" she cried. **ZING!**

Romeo's giant gadget trapped the heroes.
"I thought it was a Robot Controller?" said Catboy.

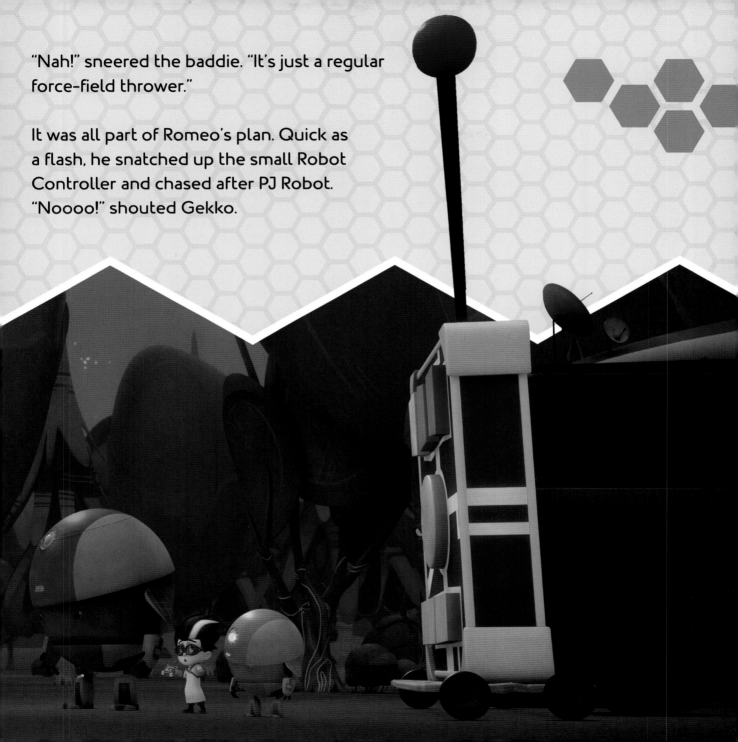

"Nah!" sneered the baddie. "It's just a regular force-field thrower."

It was all part of Romeo's plan. Quick as a flash, he snatched up the small Robot Controller and chased after PJ Robot. "Noooo!" shouted Gekko.

Romeo trapped PJ Robot but he refused to go back to the baddie. "Can you see that?" said Catboy. "He's fighting off being controlled!" "He wants to be on our team!" cheered Gekko. Owlette shouted, "Please join us, PJ Robot!"

PJ Robot broke away, then jumped into Romeo's Lab and started the engine. The Lab lurched forwards, breaking the force-field around the PJ Masks.
The heroes were free!
"So long, Romeo!" grinned Gekko.

Romeo turned to his other robot helpers.
"Attack, you metal heads!"
"No," said Robot. "I, too, do not wish to be controlled."

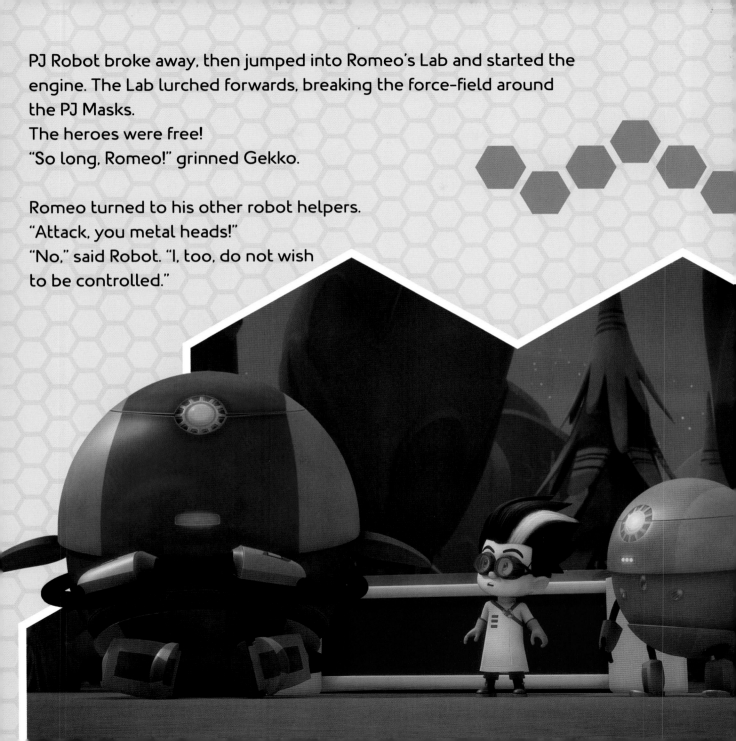

Romeo was furious, but it was too late.

"We'll meet again!" he shouted, as he disappeared into the night.

"We sure will," promised Gekko.

The PJ Masks hugged their new friend.

"PJ Robot, welcome to the team!"

PJ MASKS ALL SHOUT HOORAY. 'CAUSE IN THE NIGHT, WE SAVED THE DAY!